# WAVEFALL

Rebecca A. Demarest

Published by WRITERLY BLISS

*http://rebeccademarest.com*

Book design by Rebecca A. Demarest

The docking klaxon sounded and Brad stopped pretending to read. After a moment, the new shift of miners disembarked; mostly rough and strung out as usual, in jumpsuits showing too much wear and with the lanky stretched appearance that comes from excessive time off-world. You didn't end up on Serinus unless you were at the end of your options—or you'd pissed off Corporate something fierce.

The Serinus Mining Colony was ancient, barely maintained, and so far out that it was hardly a line-item on Corporate's balance sheet, a rounding error totalling one asteroid. That's why Brad had requested this posting. Here, his past could stay in the past; it was easier to pretend he was just another down-on-his-luck miner. It also helped that the station was small enough that it only rated one Canary, which meant that they were easier to avoid, easier to keep from thinking about his mother every time they crossed paths. The Canary for the last deployment had been an older man by the name of Davies, but he was approaching retirement, and the new Canary was due to dock in the next hour. It was this impending arrival that had Brad loitering by the docking bays during his free time, instead of gaming with his shift in the dining hall. If he knew what the new Canary looked like, it made it that much easier to stay out of their way.

The last few people through the hatch were laughing, jockeying for a spot around someone much shorter. One of them stopped and offered a hand to his shorter companion to help them over the bulkhead, and Brad got a good look at the new Canary.

Slapping the man playfully on the shoulder, she brushed past him, acting miffed at his chivalry. He gasped at the playful hit, acting like it was a mortal wound before catching back up. She had the telltale implant and heterochromia—one tawny brown eye, the other jade green—and thick dark-blonde hair wound up into a regulation bun to keep it out of the way of station instruments. Linking arms with a couple of the men, the new Canary demanded a drink.

Brad blinked a couple of times and then shook his head at their exuberance before he headed back to his quarters. This Canary was not what he had been expecting, and he wondered what exactly she had done to piss off Corporate so bad that they sent her all the way out here, because people as attractive and charismatic as that never ran out of options.

o▬  ▬o  ▬o o  o▬o  o  o▬

Andrea left her shipmates at the bar, turning down the offers of more drinks by pleading a desire to get a good night's sleep before reporting for duty. As if her antici-palpitations would let her sleep. For the first time since she was discovered hiding in plain sight, lives depended on her, on her premature coma and/ or death. The nightmares about lying paralyzed while people died around her anyway would not go away, no matter how many drugs or therapies the orientation counselors had tried.

She thought she had hated having to hide her whole life, always remember her contacts, but the reality of being a Canary and of having other human lives dependent on her was so much worse.

There was nothing she could do about that now, however. Her only way to make sure her nightmares didn't become reality was to make enough friends that they'd pause long enough to think to pick her up when she went down. And in the meantime, she'd recruit enough bed partners that when she woke up, sweating and heart pounding, there was a warm body beside her to anchor her to the here and now.

When she finally made it to her cabin, it was the size of her closet at home, but she was lucky enough to have it all to herself. There was some theory that this reduced cortical stress levels and made the implant more effective, but she hadn't been able to follow the science. She was just grateful for the end result.

Before slumping into bed, Andrea leaned toward the mirror, trying to get a good look at the "quantum implantable microtubule monitor" in her temple. The doc had declared it healed and ready for travel weeks ago, but it still itched. On the upside, these new implants meant that she didn't need to be under direct observation all the time to carry out her responsibilities; if she started to ride the Wave—or "experience catatonia with cataleptic features" as the scientists kept correcting her—the implant could read the change in her neural microtubules and automatically send out a distress beacon. On the downside, the exposed metal and light of the antenna system was disconcerting. The Canaries all knew they could make the antenna subcutaneous, and the rumor was this made it easier to dismiss us as tools, just another part of the station equipment.

But as the recruiter reminded her, it was an honor to serve the Corporation like this, just think of how many lives you are going to save, and no, you do not have a choice in the matter. When her parents had conceived her, the act of fertilization implied consent to subsection 347 of the User Agreement, which gave Corporate full authority to recruit and train Andrea the moment her Canary gene was observed.

Tomorrow, she would sync her implant with the station computers and her life would become utterly monotonous, if the stars were aligned. No drinking, no drugs, no excessive manual labor, just a regimen of light exercise and healthy food to ensure her health as the sole Canary aboard the station. All the rules were designed to keep her as physically healthy as possible until it was time for her to die. Thank the gods sex counted as light exercise.

≡ o o o  o ≡ o  o ≡  ≡ o o

Brad picked up his breakfast tray at the food line and settled into his usual corner with the novel that had arrived for him in yesterday's mail delivery. A crescendo in the noise of the room drew his attention out of his book to the Canary—and the antics at every table as they tried to entice her to join them. He snorted at them and buried his face back in his book.

A moment later a tray clattered down onto his table, startling him out of the story.

"Do you mind?" The question was entirely rhetorical as she pulled out a chair and sat down.

Just what he needed to start his day. "Uh, I'd really rather just read, if you don't mind. Are you sure you don't want to sit at one of the other tables?"

"No, this is perfect. You read. I'll ignore you and mainline this coffee. I don't want to deal with anybody before this cup is empty."

Brad opened his mouth to respond, but she held up a finger in warning. He shrugged and went back to his book. The Canary was good to her word, not uttering a single thing until her plate was clear and she had drained the last of the cup of coffee.

Setting the mug down with a thunk, she sighed. "What kind of lousy joint only allows you one cup of coffee a day? I mean, really."

"Take it up with Corporate. They're the ones who sign the supply orders." Brad tried to show his disinterest in the conversation by holding his book up higher in front of his face, but she wasn't having any of it.

"I'm Andrea."

"Brad." He held the book up a little bit higher.

She studied him for a moment before crossing her arms and leaning back. "You don't like me. But you don't know me. Which means you either hate women or Canaries. Which is it?"

"The only people who end up out here are desperate, or troublemakers. Which is it?" he returned, too irritated to try to be polite. Perhaps if he was rude enough she would leave him be.

"I stole a transpo during orientation to try and escape; turns out I can't fly. Good thing there are so few of us that they can't execute us, but they sure can send us to stations that will bore us to death. Now, is it because I'm a woman or a Canary?"

Brad sighed and closed his book, carefully marking his spot. "If you have to have a reason, it's because you're a Canary." The bell rang and he got up, tucking his book into a pocket. "No offense. I'm sure you're perfectly nice, but I've got a bad history with Canaries. Now, if you'll excuse me, I'm don't want to be late for my shift."

She waved him away. "Fine, go. See if I care."

Andrea watched Brad head out toward the shafts, keeping a discreet distance between himself and the rest of the miners. He was different from the rest of them; for one thing, he read. Most of these Neanderthals weren't even literate, depending on the holos for entertainment. Unless she had been mistaken, Brad had tucked away a paperback compendium of Sherlock Holmes after breakfast. Antiquated, but classic. If anyone was going to provide some decent conversation on this station, it was going to be him. Maybe she could bribe him with the T.S. Eliot she had stashed in her luggage. There weren't many people left who enjoyed paper books, but those who did tended to have more in common than not.

She waited until the room cleared before returning her own breakfast tray and going in search of the infirmary.

"You're late." Canary Davies scowled at her as she came through the hatch. Doctor al-Mufti looked up briefly to acknowledge her presence with a nod before returning to her computer.

Andrea hopped up onto the exam table next to Davies and drummed her feet against its base. "What's the rush? A few minutes here or there makes no difference to the machines."

"Welcome to Serinus, Canary Driscoll." The doctor grinned and shook Andrea's hand before starting to plug both Canaries into the main computer, ignoring their chatter as she worked.

"Andrea, please. I hate the title."

The doctor treated her to another sunny smile. "Imani. Now hold still…"

"This is your duty and your job, treat it with the punctuality and decorum it deserves. Now, I am done being the fool Canary on this dead rock; every minute of freedom counts to me." Davies slapped the doctor's hands away and adjusted the connection himself and Imani rolled her eyes.

"What this is, is a draft. I didn't volunteer, but when the options are active duty, research, or jail, I chose the least invasive option." She shuddered at the memory of the surgery that implanted her tech, a surgery that required the patient be fully awake while they drilled into her skull.

Davies gave a bark of laughter. "Least invasive. Jail. I get it. Good one. Maybe these miners won't make mincemeat out of you after all."

The computer chimed and uttered a soft, "Canary synced."

As Imani started unhooking them, Andrea hesitated before asking, softly, "Has it ever been here?"

The doctor paused and Davies sobered. "No. Some stations have gotten hit three, four, five times, but Serinus has been spared."

The two Canaries instinctually kissed their thumbs for luck, hoping to ward off the Wave with superstition since science was no help, but Imani turned back away to her instruments, her shoulders hunched. Andrea followed up with the question that had been really bothering her. "How do we know the implant actually works, that we're not just some human placebo?"

"Corporate says so, don't they? It's saving lives on other stations, so they say. Gotta trust them on that since I've never been close to the damn fool thing, thank all that is holy." Davies glanced at the doctor, hunched over her computer and dropped his voice to murmur to Andrea. "Doc lost her whole family on a research station. Parents, siblings...she was a teenager and happened to be playing hooky in the oxygen chamber. Their Canary was sick." He clapped a hand on Andrea's shoulder and hopped off the table, giving an abbreviated bow to the doctor. "Miss, it's been a pleasure." He headed out the hatch, leaving the doctor to unhook Andrea.

When Imani was done, Andrea said, "It wasn't his place to tell me that. But you have my condolences." This was the worst part of being a Canary, meeting people whose lives had been irrevocably altered by the Wave, knowing she was their safety net but hating every second of it. It was some pretty epic cognitive dissonance, with a good ol' helping of guilt.

"I don't mind, actually. I prefer the Canaries in my charge to know; that way you won't complain about how solicitous I can be of your health." The doctor took a deep breath, settling her shoulders, and her voice returned to its previous brisk cheerfulness. "I spend a lot of my free time reading up on the science we have about the Wave, even got one of the monitoring implants on the black market. No antenna, just the monitor." She tapped her head. "If the Wave hits, I want to be able to collect my own data on how us non-Canaries respond, as well as whatever comes out of your monitor. See if there's anything significant."

Andrea gaped at her. "That's...gods, you underwent that surgery willingly?"

"It helps to feel like I'm contributing to a solution, any way I can." Imani shrugged, and made an abrupt conversational pivot. "But that's enough dire talk for now. Is there anything I can help you with? Gossip, directions, survival tips in the canteen?"

After taking a second to reorient herself, Andrea smiled at the other woman. "I don't suppose you know the miner Brad, do you? Likes his books."

Imani's raised her eyebrows and leaned in conspiratorially. "That's Brad Lleu. You know...Little Brad Lleu?"

Andrea frowned, racking her brain for the reference. "I don't think I do."

The doctor lowered her voice even more. "He's the boy who lived."

"I'm pretty sure that was Harry Potter." The doctor stared blankly at Andrea. "You know, digi-modern classical children's literature? The wizard? Nevermind."

Imani waved her hand dismissively. "I prefer holos. Brad is that Canary's son, the only one who survived the Wave when it hit Station Epsilon back in the beginning of the Canary Service, before the implants. He used to catch a lot of flack about not hitting the alarm before he took shelter, especially from anyone who had relatives on that station—and it was a really big station. There isn't so much trouble anymore, thankfully. Mostly people have forgotten."

Andrea's lips quirked up into a half smile. "And things start to make sense." She jumped off the table, stretching. "Hey, I don't know if you're interested, but I brought some stuff from the Core, a sort of friendship bribe. Trinkets, but pretty, and some sweets. You want me to bring them by at shift change so you can pick out your favorite bits?"

The doc gave her a spontaneous hug. "Oh, I will absolutely take you up on that. Now go acquaint yourself with our meager outpost on this rock. I've got paperwork to do."

Andrea spent the rest of her first shift exploring the station, including poking her head into the holo control room where the miners piloted their rigs via VR. The thirty men on shift were suspended in full rigs around the room, communicating via dermal throat mics that kept the room eerily quiet.

The shift captain noticed Andrea standing in the doorway and kicked her out before she got in the way of a rig swinging around. The equipment the men were using was robust, but expensive. Any distractions, even her bumping into a rig, could have monetary consequences. Andrea continued through the station, finding the station master's office and her other non-grunt female companion, Stacy, to whom she extended the same invitation as the doctor. She found the gym, the tiny commissary, the holosuites, identified and avoided the miners' barracks by the stench of body odor, before finally stopping by the canteen for a piece of fruit. She chatted with the cook for a short while, offering her assistance during her copious amounts of free time, then left him to his lunch preparations. She took her apple back to the door in the station she had already walked by twice in her explorations, but had yet to open.

You couldn't miss it, what with the giant red arrows on every wall pointing the way to the door. If you were headed out into space, you were repeatedly informed that if you heard the alarm, you followed the red. Period. Don't hesitate, just go. If you were a Canary, they told you something different: you'd never hear the alarm because you'd already be as good as dead.

In some ways it was comforting. She'd go catatonic, never aware of what was happening, and by the time the Wave had passed, she would be dead or her body disappeared, just like anyone else who didn't make it into this room. There is no way to detect the Wave except through the cognitive effect it had on a small portion of the population with a random genetic mutation. Some resonant interference on the quantum level with a structure in the brain that lived on the same gene mutation as heterochromia. Even that much was only discovered by accident.

Thirty years ago, a man with heterochromia—the first Canary—went catatonic and, luckily, he was part of the medical crew. When he collapsed in the med bay, he was under recorded observation for the last seven minutes before the Wave hit. The Canary was dead and the rest of the crew was missing by the time the previously summoned med-rescue shuttle arrived, but after a few more years of study and gene sequencing, Earth was happy to announce that there was finally a way to tell if the Wave was approaching. And all it cost was the life of a Canary whose name no one even remembered.

The second discovery during this era was that certain kinds of superconducting materials could protect crew members from the Wave. A research station had a small room designed with a Deutsch cage—named for the quantum scientist David Deutsch—to shield its contents from every possible source of contamination: radiation, electrical, q-bit, and theoretical. Two scientists were updating the experiments in the room at the same time that their station was hit by the Wave and while they fell unconscious, they survived. The material was expensive and made communications impossible, so instead of shielding entire ships and stations, each ship had their bioreactors retrofitted with inlaid walls of the material, usually sourced from asteroid mines like Serinus.

Canaries weren't allowed to cross the threshold of the safe room. Ever. If they went in, signals from their implant couldn't get out, and in the event of Wavefall the station would have no warning. Andrea stood outside the red door for a few minutes, staring at the push handle, the only door on the station designed without any kind of latch or lock so that nothing would prevent the crew from entering. After a couple deep breaths, she opened the door to stare into the bioengineered jungle inside. She could barely make out the strips of metal along the inside walls, glinting orange through the foliage.

During orientation, she asked one of their instructors, "Does anyone ever try to get the Canaries to safety before Wavefall? I mean, once they collapse, couldn't they be carried into the oxygen chamber? Our job is done at that point."

"Oh, they always say they will." The instructor smiled, and Andrea could tell by the wry twist to their lips just how many crews actually kept that promise. "But even if by some miracle you do end up in the cage, don't expect to survive there either. It's only 50/50 whether you'll recover from the catatonia. We tried offering a reward to bring the Canaries into the safe room, but that never seemed to override humanity's desire to take care of themselves first. They figure you're most likely going to die anyway, so why bother risking it? Best to just always keep your affairs in order."

Andrea let the door to the oxygen chamber swing shut, and it bounced heavily against its frame, leaving her with one last gust of fresh air before the station's environmental system sucked the scent of green and growing things out of the hallway. Roughly, she wiped the tears off her face before marching back to her bunk to read until the end of her assigned "day" shift when she would have access to the rec areas again and could distract herself by playing the flirt. She really didn't want to spend the night alone.

≡ o o o  o ≡ o  o ≡  ≡ o o

Disconnecting from his VR rig, Brad rolled his shoulders to try and work out some of the tension from the last few hours of mining before following his cohort to the canteen. Exhausted from the concentration the rig required of him, he was not paying attention when someone stepped into line behind him.

"Heya!" Andrea tapped him lightly on his shoulder.

Brad's heart leapt into his throat and he spun a little too fast, narrowly avoided clipping Andrea with his upraised arm, angled to defend his face. She backed up quickly, hands up. "Easy there, tiger. Just trying to say hello."

It took a few deep breaths before Brad could lower his arm. "Sorry, it's my fault. I'm always jumpy coming out of the rig. And, well..." He shrugged. "I'm used to having to defend myself."

She gave him an appraising look up and down and Brad found himself flushing with embarrassment, even though her regard was more clinical than lustful, clocking his lean figure kept in shape by hours in the rig. "Well, you look like you can defend yourself just fine. But you have nothing to fear from me." She gestured to her five-foot frame. "I can't even reach the top shelf in my bunk."

Brad couldn't help but smile, but only a little. "I somehow doubt you're the helpless little lady you pretend to be."

She grinned. "Well, maybe I'm just trying to make sure you big burly men will remember to drag my catatonic ass to the cage during Wavefall. I certainly don't weigh enough to slow any of you down."

He almost missed the sadness in her eyes, but from one faker to another, he recognized the mask Andrea had just put on. He did her the courtesy of ignoring her true feelings and accepted her diversion. "Trust me, at the rate you're making friends, you'll be fine. About half these grunts will do anything for the company of a skirt. The rest are happy with their bunkmates but they're still desperate for up-to-date news from the Core. Stay away from Lewis, though—he gets clingy." He turned around to grab a tray and started pulling plates from the serving line. "Hey, look! They pulled out all the stops to welcome you, it's leftover casserole."

Andrea laughed, grinning at him before waving to the cook. The cook handed her a large salad made with fresh greens from the hydroponics bays and topped with an assortment of nuts, fruits, and a delicately sliced meat.

Brad raised an eyebrow. "What the stars is that?"

"I have food sensitivities on top of the special Canary diet, so I stopped by to have a chat with Giorgio here earlier today. I brought him some of my replacement foods and a few gifts from home. He's agreed to make sure I'm eating well. Thank you, Giorgio, you're a dear." Andrea walked over to the seating area and played eeny-meeny-miny-moe with a handful of tables clamoring for her attention before sitting down at one that hadn't even been in the running. She flipped off the men catcalling her from the other tables, shoved a few men aside and claimed her seat.

Shaking his head at her brass, Brad turned to grab his own plates and was met with a mini version of her salad instead of the standard wilted greens normally served to the miners. Giorgio smiled at him. "She said if there was extra, you could have it if you promised to share your books. She also said you wouldn't listen if it was her asking, so she wanted me to do it for her."

"She does have a way with people, doesn't she?" Brad considered the colorful salad being offered to him, shrugged, and took it. He looked back at the table Andrea had conquered and found her watching him, one eyebrow raised, so he toasted her with the salad, then turned back to grab casserole as well. "So, what can't she eat?"

Shaking his head, Giorgio barked with laughter. "Cafeteria food, apparently."

Brad took his meal to the quietest corner he could and pulled out his book, but found himself paying more attention to Andrea than to the plot. He had to admit, she was charismatic. She had the miners laughing and chattering, without any of the reservation they usually showed around other new folks on station. She actually listened to the stories they were telling her, and her food disappeared with alacrity from her plate. And a few of her neighbors' plates as well. She used the cover of cracking a joke to sneak the extra roll off the plate to her left, and covered it well in butter before disappearing that down her gullet as well.

The miners lingered over their empty plates for a while before heading off to the holosuites, though she turned down an invitation to join them. She whispered something into one of their ears before they left, and the miner actually blushed! Unfortunately, Brad had gotten to know these men well; there wasn't anything he'd found yet that could make them blush. Except for her.

Andrea slapped Matt on the back as he left, looking forward to a decent tumble later that night, then wandered over to Brad's table. He hurriedly turned his attention back to his book. She'd seen him watching her all evening and his concerted effort to avoid her eye amused her. "I see you accepted my peace salad. Does this mean we have a truce?"

Brad poked a loaded fork at her, dressing dripping. "Peace salad! That explains the taste of self-righteousness."

She laughed, sitting in the empty chair across from him. "I'm afraid that's all you, bud. Must have bitten your lip. This salad tastes of friendship and good books. I've got a T.S. Eliot if you want it. And a couple others. Trade you for those Holmes stories when you're done."

Brad stuffed the forkful of salad into his mouth, chewing slowly and swallowing before answering. "You know you can read those stories on tablet, right?"

"But why would I do that when I can hold and smell the book in my hands? Also, it won't run out of batteries, unlike the rest of the entertainment I brought from Earth to fill the lonely times." Brad choked on his salad as Andrea smirked. "Stand to hear a bit more?"

Brad shook his head as he cleared his windpipe. "Nope. All set over here."

Waiting until Brad took a drink of water, she responded with: "Good, cause I have to go meet the other ladies in my bunk for a party." Andrea laughed as water sprayed, before getting up and prancing out of the cafeteria.

Once she knew she was out of sight, she slumped against the wall, rubbing her eyes. She had accomplished her mission of cementing herself as a source of fun for the crew; even Brad was warming up. Though with his history, gods only know how he'd respond if the Wave did fall. When she heard footsteps coming down the hall, she stood up, adjusted her smile to full wattage, and continued to her bunk to start bribing the women of the station for their good regard.

▬ ₀₀₀  ₀▬₀  ₀▬  ▬₀₀

The next morning, Brad was already in his favorite corner table when Andrea came in, followed closely by Matt. The hulking miner tried to say something to her, but she waved him to silence, grabbed a tray of food and coffee, and found her way to Brad's table, leaving Matt to his friends.

Remembering the previous morning, Brad simply nodded to her in greeting, then ignored her while she studiously cleared her plate and emptied her mug. When it was dry, she inverted it onto her plate and rested her forehead on the bottom of the mug. She mumbled something too quiet for Brad to hear. "I didn't quite catch that."

Andrea groaned and pulled herself upright enough to prop her chin in her hand. "Decaf. Giorgio is apparently unable to be bribed to even give me real coffee now that I'm your stupid Canary. How am I supposed to live?"

"Apparently sleepily. Also, it would seem congrats are in order." Brad turned back to his book, hoping to finish the chapter before his shift started.

Struggling to keep her eyes open and focused, her only reply was, "Hmm?"

Brad nodded toward the group of miners listening with rapt attention and raunchy interjections to Matt's obvious rendition of the night, complete with miming. "Your exploits will soon be spread across the whole of the station. Looks like he had a good time."

Andrea groaned at the effort it took to turn her head and look. After watching the pantomime for a few moments, she snorted, but smiled. "Eh, he's good enough in the sack; I'll let him have his moment. If he gets annoying, all I have to do is start telling them all about the tattoo on his ass."

"Which is..." Brad prompted.

"Oh, no you don't. That's my leverage if Matt tries to make things weird. All he's doing right now is expanding the pool of interested suitors to keep me entertained in this hellhole." Andrea picked up her mug and stared soulfully into it. "All I have left is endorphins to keep me happy, so it's either exercise or sex. They won't let me exercise much either, which means I'm going to spend my morning doing dishes in order to keep myself from going stark raving mad."

"Thank your stars that you're not stuck in a rig all day, staring at identical sections of rock on your screen." Brad noted the time and started to clean up. Andrea still held her mug, staring as though she could will coffee into it if she just tried hard enough. "Look, at least you don't have to spend all your shifts in an observation tank like they used to, right? You've got free range of the station. Go spend some time in the holosuites."

Andrea wrinkled her nose and finally set her mug down. "If I'm stuck in a cage, I'd rather be able to see the bars."

Brad shrugged and walked away with his tray, thinking about that time not so long ago that he'd lived with his mother in an observation suite. She was only under observation for twelve hours a day because the computer couldn't tell the difference between a Wave fit and sleep back then, so there were always two Canaries at the critical stations: one awake with people, cameras, and computers watching, and one asleep. He remembered his mother telling him to just ignore the cameras in the corners of the room, and the occasional beep from the system when she had been still for too long and the observational software needed to be sure she was still responsive to her environment. He'd hated the feeling of being trapped and watched, and would run away from the room as often as he could when the little red lights indicated her shift was active. It hadn't stopped her from dying, and it sure as hell hadn't kept the station from being emptied. He tried to put it out of his mind as he headed to his rig.

Andrea waited for the canteen to empty before heading behind the food lines to help Giorgio with the morning dishes. It was the work of a few moments to scrape all the leftovers into the recycler so their matter could be reduced and reused around the station, and easy enough to load the plates into the sanitizer. The chore didn't take as much time as she'd hoped, so she went up to the administrative offices to draft a letter to home.

It was expensive to send communications from this far out back to the inner planets, but everybody on station was given a quota of data each quarter to send updates to their families at home. There was no restriction on incoming data since the senders footed the bill, so there was usually a steady stream of information about what was going on at home, even if it was a few months late.

The station master was happy to see her and activated the message recording booth, a private-ish corner of the office with a recorder and simple interface designed to make the encoding and compression of the message simple. She tapped the appropriate buttons to send to one of her favorited addresses and splurged the extra credits for video as well as audio recording, at least for this first message home. She smiled a couple times before starting the recording, making sure she had her best face forward. No sense worrying the folks back home.

"Hey Mom, Dad. So, I made it to Sirinus alright, the flight out was long and boring, but now I get to be even more bored! Just kidding. The station is actually really nice, they've got good amenities out here, several holosuites. Everyone here is friendly, especially the two other ladies on board with me. One's admin, the other's the doc, and they were really appreciative of my gifts, so thanks for the suggestions, Mom. Been entertaining myself helping out with the chores I'm allowed to pitch in on and catching up on my reading."

She wanted to add, "sitting and waiting to die," but didn't think her parents would appreciate that part.

"I know you did your best to keep me away from this life, and I appreciate it. At the very least I wasn't forced into the program as a kid, so thanks for that. Hopefully you'll be wrapping up your mandated customer service punishment rotation soon. I sometimes wonder if I made the right choice in submitting to the Canary program, if I shouldn't have fought to stay out of it harder, but alea iacta est, right, Dad? Anyway, I'm about to run out of credits, so I love you, I miss you, and I hope I'll be rotated off this rock soon." Andrea blew a kiss to the camera, waved goodbye and ended the recording. She hit the compress and queue buttons, and her message was ready to go out with the next communications burst.

She sat there for a moment more, steeling herself to go out and flirt with Bill and chat with Stacy. "Make as many friends as you can," her mother had advised her. "But don't come across as desperate." Her father had added, "The more friends you make, the more likely you are to survive." Considering they had both served time as deployed Canaries, Andrea knew they were right. Her mother had even survived an encounter with the Wave because she had collapsed directly into the arms of her best friend. Her parents told that story a lot because what they didn't know at the time was that she was already pregnant with Andrea.

Providence smiled on her parents and her mother was given a year's leave to recuperate after the incident, which meant she managed to hide her pregnancy and birth from start to finish. Female Canaries weren't supposed to get pregnant, but she had fallen in love with another of the Canaries in her cohort and life will find a way. Andrea's parents had managed to keep her hidden from Corporate by having an aunt raise her, and there were always colored contacts to keep people from noticing her telltale eye coloration. But one slip-up in front of a college boyfriend and one bad breakup later, Corporate found out she was heterochromic. It only took them two days to come collect her.

When the Canary draft had begun, human rights lawyers tried to get involved to stop Corporate from press-ganging anyone with the chromosomal abnormality into their flock of disposable humans, but they failed miserably. Every human signed a User Agreement when they had any sort of contact with Corporate, and there was no way to avoid the agreement unless you lived in an unmapped corner of the world. Even then, you probably had to sign one in order to get transport there. And buried in every User Agreement was a line giving Corporate blanket permission to use you as needed for "the good of all mankind." Surviving the Wave was considered one such situation, and so the human rights lawyers lost. In a magnanimous gesture, Corporate agreed to pay Canaries and their families an astoundingly high salary and death benefits, as well as fund research into ways to replace the human component. Thus far, they had been unsuccessful.

That left Andrea stuck on this damned asteroid, waiting for Wavefall. She would have made a deal with the devil himself to have a drink right now.

━ ◦◦◦  ◦ ━ ◦  ◦ ━  ━ ◦◦

Brad cursed as his rig shuddered, informing him that he had missed his mark. Again. "Lleu!" the shift leader hollered in his ear. "I need you here, you bastard. That machine is worth more than five of you together!" He'd been trying to shake off his funk all shift, but it was sometimes hard to get his brain to stop repeating his world's-worst-moments montage when he was stuck in the mind-numbing rig. You make one terrified decision as a child and the holos would be sure it haunted you for the rest of your life. There was even some badly produced real-life-story holo about the whole thing with a burned-out child actor (now dead of an OD) sobbing Brad's part. Poorly. In reality, he hadn't cried at all. He'd felt too numb and simply done what his mother had coached him to do repeatedly. He got into the box.

He still had it, the trunk his mother had retrofitted with the Deutsch cage she had paid dearly for. It was an antique steamer trunk, specially outfitted with little shutters that could be unlocked from the inside to allow airflow. If he'd been strong enough he probably could have fit his mother into the box with him, but he was only twelve, she was catatonic, and she had made him promise—promise—that if she ever went down he wouldn't hesitate. He would go straight into the box. And he did. The last thing he remembered before losing consciousness was staring out at her slack face from between the strips of orange metal forming the Deutsch cage.

Taking a breath to focus himself, Brad brought his attention to bear on the asteroid in front of him. The giant version of the rig was out in space, a monster 100 times the size he was, and bristling with the newest tech. If he broke it, he'd never work off the debt.

After his shift concluded with no more lapses in attention, he declined to follow his shift mates to the mess hall and headed to his bunk before dinner. Reaching under his bed, he dragged out the trunk that had saved his life. No matter how many bad memories were associated with the thing, he found the idea of getting rid of it panic-inducing, so he always made sure he could pay the extra luggage cost to bring it along. He could even still fit in it if he squeezed. He opened it (now full of his clothing and odds and ends) and toggled the locks that kept the little windows closed, checking that they still opened freely.

Staring into the trunk started to make him feel claustrophobic, so he latched it all back up and shoved it under his bed before heading out to dinner.

Andrea saw Brad come into the dining hall and slip into his spot without once looking over to where she held court. She was miffed he didn't say hello, but it wasn't like she was lacking for company. Turning her attention back to the rig pilot beside her, she leaned in conspiratorially to hear his whispered punchline, and laughed as was expected. Over the course of the meal, she thought she caught Brad looking her direction every once in a while, so she laughed harder and talked louder than she otherwise might. The men at the table couldn't tell the difference, since they were getting progressively louder as their end-of-shift booze rations took hold. The next time she looked up, he was gone, his place cleared.

The next morning when she went to sit with him over her silent breakfast, she was brought up short by the fact that his table was empty.

She went back to the chow line. "Hey, Giorgio, is Brad sick?"

The genial man glanced at Brad's usual corner while wiping down the chow line with a rag. "Naw, came in earlier, ate quick, left."

"Huh." She decided to go to the table anyway, since she still didn't feel like being social, but she missed the quiet comradeship. After she finished, Andrea puttered through her day in what was becoming her usual fashion: helping Giorgio in the kitchen, seeing if there was anything she could do in the admin office, wandering the station, putting in her mandatory two hours of light physical activity, and reading in the tidy little nest she'd put together by one of the rare viewports. When dinner finally came around, she eagerly made her way back to the canteen and her harem of men. Brad finally showed up, but once again ignored her, ate quickly, then got out just as fast. She was now certain he was avoiding her.

The pattern held for several days. He'd be done with breakfast before she managed to make it to the canteen (though given how hard it was for her to get going in the morning, that wasn't terribly surprising) but he would also ignore her entirely at dinner. After the meal, he'd disappear.

Finally, she was fed up with his behavior and excused herself from dinner as he left the hall. She caught up to him in the deserted passageway and called out to him. "Brad! Brad! Stop a second, will you?"

He glanced over his shoulder, sighed, but stopped. He crossed his arms as he turned to meet her. "Yes?"

Andrea noted the defensive posture and gave him more than the usual personal space. "Look, did I do something to offend you?"

"I would think you have enough friends back there already, why bother with one more?" He started to turn away, but Andrea slipped in front of him, her anger outweighing her confusion for the moment. She stopped him with a firm hand to the chest.

"Oh my gods, are you jealous? Wake up man, it's the future. A girl can be friends with whomever, and sleep with whomever she wants, guy, girl, in-between, neither. You didn't strike me as a back-century prude."

He finally uncrossed his arms and put his hands on his hips. "I am not a prude. I don't care if you sleep your way through the whole station. No, I'm not jealous. I just...it's hard to be around you, okay? For once, it genuinely is me, not you. Canaries and I don't have the best track record so I try to stay as far away from them—you—as I can. But just because I like you—"

"Hah! I knew it!" Andrea crowed.

He threw his hands in the air. "Oh my god, grow up. Just because I thought you were a more interesting conversationalist than the rest of the miners on station, don't think I'm going to start pining over you like that lot." He started walking away, and Andrea hurried to catch up.

"I just think you'd change your mind if we actually spent some time together, is all, instead of you eating and running every meal. That's got to be starting to give you indigestion..." Andrea trailed off and Brad didn't realize she'd dropped behind for a moment. He turned to face her, a rebuke about respecting boundaries on his lips when he noticed her expression.

"Andrea? Are you okay?" Brad returned to her side.

There was a faint noise, just past the edge of her hearing, that was niggling at her consciousness and she turned her head back and forth trying to pinpoint it, but it stayed constant regardless of where she was facing. "Do you hear that?" No, it wasn't constant after all, it was growing louder, but from where?

Brad sighed. "It's a space station, there's all sorts of noise."

"It's...singing? Like whale song. Really, how can you not hear it? It's getting so loud now." Andrea covered her ears but it didn't help. There was a pattern in the sound, and it was almost like she could almost hear words in the wave of sound, see images...

She stopped, and looked up at the silent alarms, horrified. "It's the Wave." She grabbed Brad and started towing him down the corridor in the direction of the red arrows.

"Stop. Come on, Andrea, what are you talking about? Don't joke about something like this." Brad pulled his arm out of her grasp and backed away. The look on his face plainly said he was pissed, and she didn't blame him. She was awake. She wasn't supposed to be awake, but with every passing moment, her certainty about what she was hearing grew.

"Look, have you ever known a Canary who was the child of two Canaries? I don't think so. Pretty sure I'm the only one in existence. And I can hear it coming. Even if you don't believe me, isn't it better to be safe than sorry?" Andrea grabbed his arm and started towing him down the hall again.

Her absolute conviction started to sway Brad, but he stopped again. "Why aren't the alarms going off? We have to set off the alarms!" He wasn't going to be the only one to survive the Wave again, even if he had to stand in the middle of the canteen and shout. Andrea cast about the hallway for a moment, then darted over to the general alert alarm and yanked.

The siren was piercing, a pulsing shriek, different than the rise and fall dragon-wail of the Wave alarm. But he knew why she did it. Most of the crew on station would immediately head to the oxygen chamber anyway since it was also the most reinforced part of the station and offered the best chance of survival. However, he caught Andrea as she started back toward the chamber.

"What? We're running out of time!" She had to yell to be heard over the siren and the rising tide of pressure in her own head.

"You can't go in there, you're not catatonic. If they see you, and no one else knows what the problem is with the station, they might leave again."

"Where else can I go?" She was shaking but whether from fear, adrenaline, or the sheer overload of the Wave in her head, she wasn't sure. She always thought she'd be blissfully unconscious for this part.

"My bunk, Barrack 5, there's a trunk. The trunk I survived in as a kid. Go!" He pushed her back down the hallway and she only hesitated for a moment before breaking and running. He made sure she was headed the right way before turning and sprinting full out for the shelter of the Deutsch cage himself, gathering people as he went, shouting, "Canary is down! Canary is down!"

Andrea made it to Barrack 5 and threw herself on the floor looking for the trunk. Catching sight of the dull metal exterior under one of the bunks, she hauled on its strap and managed to yank it out from under the bed. Throwing up the lid, she growled and started dumping stuff out. Precious moments, precious moments. She could tell it was almost on top of them: the singing in her head made her teeth ache and she thought she would burst from the pressure of it. No wonder Canaries went catatonic, if this is what they heard. And yet, her implant was dormant. She was awake.

She stepped into the newly emptied trunk, popped the window locks, knelt down—

And paused.

The Wave crested over the station and something touched her mind. It was the only way she could describe it. She felt another mind, a presence and consciousness not her own brush the edges of her own awareness. It was intimate, like a 4 a.m. conversation with your best friend, where you are both perfectly in sync, but there was so much information that poured into her that she couldn't track it. All she could do was watch the cascade of data slipping past her mind's eye, and even that was almost too much. She was going to drown in the waterfall of it.

"Please, no," she whispered.

The music paused, hiccuped in its patterns, and she dropped into the trunk and let the lid drop shut on top of her.

▬ ° ° °  ° ▬ °  ° ▬  ▬ ° °

A brief headcount showed that all but a couple of the miners had made it to the oxygen chamber safely, and everyone was waking up, albeit slowly. Brad stayed right where he was while people shook feeling back into their limbs. Not everybody had made it to the ground before they lost consciousness, and one guy had a broken nose, but everybody else seemed to be in decent shape. Nobody expected to be able to find the two missing miners; bodies were rarely left behind.

The low murmur of the crew checking in with each other was interrupted by a minder crying out. "Why didn't the Wave alarm go off? Is something wrong with our Canary? I don't want to die out in the ass-end of nowhere!"

He was calmed by the men around him, and their shift leader turned to Brad. "You saw the Canary go down, right?"

To give himself a moment, Brad rubbed his eyes and struggled to a kneeling position. He hesitated at revealing Andrea's unique reaction to the Wave, unsure how the men around him would take it. He'd seen them turn unreasonable and fearful over far less interesting information. "I don't really know. All I know is the Canary collapsed right in front of me and then I started running, but the alarm wasn't going off, so I tripped the general alarm." He found it disturbing that no one had used her name yet, not even Matt or the other men who had slept with her. "Look, Andrea's in my cabin, we can find out." Brad hauled himself upright with the help of a tree branch and worked his way unsteadily to the door.

The walk felt longer than usual, but he and half the station personnel made it to Barrack 5 and popped the door manually since the electronic door controls were still out. Brad sighed in relief when he saw his trunk in the middle of the room and his stuff scattered around it. Andrea had made it. He opened the lid to find her unconscious and curled into a tight little ball, blood all over her face. Concerned, he checked first for a pulse (present), then any wounds (none) so he said over his shoulder, "She's good. She hit her nose on the way down, but I put her in here to stay safe during the Wave. It's lined."

"You took the time to get her in here." Lewis helped Brad lift Andrea out of the trunk since it was obvious she wasn't going to be waking up immediately.

Brad started gently massaging Andrea's wrists, trying to wake her up. "Trust me, I know exactly how long it takes to get from my bunk to the safe room and I also know exactly how long it takes from the moment of catatonia to Wavefall. I had the time, so I took it. I didn't think carrying her through the station was the best idea at the time; unconscious people are difficult to manhandle without injury, which you should remember from our last vacation leave."

Lewis shook his head, but took Andrea's other wrist and copied Brad's gentle ministrations. After a few moments, Andrea's eyes fluttered open. She was silent at first, but lifted one blood-covered hand to her face before letting out a small, "Oh." Her bloodshot eyes flitted across the small crowd of people around her and she smiled, just a little bit. "Looks like I made it through," she whispered.

After a moment, her eyes widened and she sat up, listing slightly as the blood rushed to her head. She grabbed Brad's hand in a desperate crush, whispering, "I know what it is. I know where it's going."

He wanted to ascribe the lurch in his stomach to post-Wave nausea, but he knew it was in response to Andrea's words. She was going to out herself in front of the crew, and there was no coming back from marking yourself different like that.

Lewis leaned in, "What was that?"

Brad shook his head, keeping the motion as small as possible before turning to Lewis. "I don't think she's feeling well, we should get her to the infirmary. Can you help me get her upright?"

Between the two of them, they got Andrea up off the floor. She still wasn't steady enough on her feet to be walking anywhere, so Brad scooped her up and maneuvered carefully out into the hall.

"My hero," Andrea mumbled, her arms locked loosely around his neck and her head buried in his shoulder.

"Don't thank me yet, we're not out of the woods. Just, keep your mouth shut, alright? Trust me, you don't want to be more of a freak if you can help it."

Andrea didn't answer, and let Brad carry her into the infirmary and laid her gently on one of the cots. Imani bustled over, plainly surprised to see the Canary alive and—if not well— mostly upright.

"Well, didn't you beat the odds." She took Andrea's vitals with quick efficiency, and hooked her up to a bag of fluids to help compensate for the amount of blood that seemed to have leaked out of her eyes, her nose, and maybe even her ears. "Now, excuse me for a moment, dear, I need to brush up on any after-effects I should be looking for when a Canary lives. It's not a common occurrence."

The doc walked away and Andrea asked the rest of the miners to leave who had followed them in with a plea for quiet and rest, and a sincere thanks for making sure she was alright. She kept her hand on Brad's arm to keep him behind.

As soon as they had the small room to themselves, Andrea leaned over to whisper to Brad. "I heard it. It's alive."

Brad shook his head, firm in his denial. "The Wave? That's impossible, it's not a thing...it's...it's energy or radiation or something. And why were you unconscious when we found you?"

She made a face. "I am pretty sure I passed out because I'm afraid of blood, not because of the Wave. Though, let me tell you, the racket it made...I almost wish I did go catatonic. That was...rough."

"Let's say I believe you, just for the moment. You're saying the Wave is an intelligent being? It doesn't show up on any of our sensors, we can't measure it, we can't track it, we've not even found a pattern in the way it moves. And yet you say you....what? Heard it?" Brad felt his anger mounting as he continued, though he knew he wasn't angry at Andrea. He was angry at himself because he didn't want to believe her. If what she was saying was true, then his mother died...well, he wasn't sure what it meant.

"I don't think we can sense it because it's..." Andrea trailed off while she racked her head, trying to describe what she sensed from the Wave. "I think it dips into our space from somewhere else."

The doc had wandered back into the infirmary from her office in time to hear the last part of their conversation. She nodded in excitement while Brad grumbled in frustration. "Like something from a dimensional space orthogonal to our own. There's a whole branch of science devoted to the idea. You said you heard something?"

"And I think it heard me, too." Andrea launched into a graphic and somewhat confused description of her experience in the few minutes leading up to Wavefall, finishing with, "I was trying to get into Brad's lined trunk and I thought my head was going to explode with the force of the information overload, so I asked it to stop. And it did. That's when I dropped into the trunk and I lost all sense of it."

"Well that should be easy enough to check." The doctor bustled over to her workstation and started to plug a cord into Andrea's cybernetics.

The Canary adjusted the cord to a more comfortable angle. "It is? How?"

"Your implant records all sorts of input that comes into your brain, gathering data to see how you lot process what's going on since we can't very well ask most of you...let's see." A dashboard popped up on her screen and Imani skimmed through several screens before pulling up some graphs. "Yes, see here, and here? Your brain was receiving an insane amount of stimulus, several areas of your cerebellum were activated, memory centers, speech centers. And the Q-bit involvement at the neural microtubule level–my gods."

Andrea struggled to sit upright and see the screen. "What, is it bad?"

"No, it's just...the q-bit involvement is off the charts. Here, look." Imani moved her hair aside and plugged her own monitor in, flipping through the data on a separate screen. "See, during Wavefall, my q-bit levels dropped to about half what they were prior to the loss of consciousness. And here." She shuffled through screens, finally finding data pulled from multiple Canary monitors from their own Wavefalls. Brad wondered how many dead people that screen represented. Dead Canaries, like his mother. "The q-bits of Canaries experiencing Wavefall all but disappear. The ones who don't die seem to retain slightly higher levels than others, but still. You? Well, look." Imani turned the screen with Andrea's data toward them. Brad studied all three, but Andrea gasped first. "Holy shit, that's...do humans normally have that much quantum...thingness going on?"

"Q-bit involvement," Imani corrected, still overly excited. "It's never been recorded this high. Ever."

Brad frowned. "But couldn't that all be her version of catatonia though? Her being a Canary squared and all?"

Imani flicked through a few more screens and pulled up another complicated chart. "No, this is definitely responses from an outside stimulus and not generated by her own brain. Here, and here, absolutely atypical for brain patterns of Canaries entering or in catatonia. Sometimes we've seen spikes similar to this activity in some Canaries right before Wavefall, but until now, they've all gone down. Maybe they did experience some form of interaction with the Wave, we'll never know for sure."

Brad continued to frown all the way through the doctor's diagnostic, but didn't question her science. Instead, he returned to Andrea's initial response upon waking up. "You said you know where it's going." If she was right, if it wasn't all just some spasm of her subconscious...getting ahead of the Wave meant saving lives.

"I remember catching just the edge of it as it paused, and I knew where it was going. It's not a random pattern. Well, it is to us, but it makes sense in...more than our dimension? If that makes sense." Andrea turned to Imani. "Can you pull up a system map in here?"

"Yes, one second." The doc went to the holo display and swiped through a few screens before pulling up the maps. "Here." She turned the display toward Andrea so she could manipulate it herself.

Muttering to herself, Andrea started rotating star maps until she found an orientation she seemed to recognize. "Not the local system, zoom out a bit. Okay, now zoom in over here. Closer. Closer. " Andrea paled as she realized where she was pointing. "Oh god. Titus. There's no way they have enough shielding for all those civilians." It only took her a moment to make a decision, to finally feel like she could fight the terror her nightmares brought. "Brad, I have to get out there, I have to try and talk to it again."

"Absolutely not," Imani snapped. "You've just been through a hellish physical ordeal, your vitals are all over the map, and given your reaction to its presence last time, how do you know it won't kill you next time? We can send a message."

"I don't know if I will survive, but I have to try! You know how we will sound if we just send a message. I need to look them in the eye, convince as many traders to take off as possible and get ahead of the Wave to try and...warn it off, or something." Andrea stood up from the hospital bed and promptly swayed.

Brad caught her, keeping her upright. "You know most of the people on independent stations can barely afford food, let alone shielding in their ships."

"The doc is right, you're in no shape to go anywhere. Plus, you told me yourself that you can't fly."

Andrea clung to his arm to keep herself upright. "No, but you can. I know you can, you've got all that time in the rig."

Brad's eyebrows snapped up and a harsh laugh escaped him. "That doesn't mean I can fly a ship. Yeah, I know rigs, but a ship..."

"Is less complex than one of those mining machines. Imani, you gotta let me go after the Wave. Maybe I can talk it into changing course." She took a risk and threw the doctor's words back at her. "I have to do what I can, for a solution. To stop people from dying. What else is a Canary for?" Andrea pulled out her IV, grimacing at the sensation.

Imani sighed, taking over bandaging Andrea's arm. "I agree. But first things first, we're sending an alert to Titus. See if we can't get as many people out of that anarchist bazaar as possible. " The doc turned to her computer and pulled up off-station messaging, entering her override. The doctor typed up a quick message, appended her credentials and coded it emergency priority. When it was sent, she turned back to Brad and Andrea. "That will still take a day to reach Titus, and I have no idea if they will believe me. How long do they have?"

Andrea paused, and then shook her head. "Soon is all I got. It's on a schedule. I think it's a scientist, or...some kind of observer.." She turned her face up to Brad, who was still supporting some of her weight. "Please. Help me stop it."

Brad stared down at Andrea, trying to keep his fear off his face. He'd spent his life running away from that first deadly encounter with the Wave and now this Canary was begging him to chase it.

It didn't take long to make a decision. This time, it was the right one, he was sure of it.

"Alright. There is a freight transpo in dock. They were scheduled to leave tomorrow, which means it should be fueled and supplied. Doc, can you get her there? I need to grab my trunk." Brad shifted his weight out from around Andrea as Imani took over supporting her.

"The transpo has a safe room, you know," the doc called as Brad started to leave.

Brad paused in the door. "Not one that will allow me to pilot till the last second. The trunk needs to be right behind me, in case she's right." He left.

"Looks like you have a knight in shining armor," the doc joked.

Andrea chuckled, pulling herself upright. "To hell with that. I'm the knight, he's my trusty steed."

o══ ══o ══oo o══o o o══

Once they reached the docking bay, it only took Imani a moment to override the transpo entry security and flight codes with her administration privileges. "It's good to be king," she said and helped Andrea on board.

A thump behind them announced Brad's entry. He slid into the pilot rig, flipped a couple switches, then settled in. "Found the tutorial, give me a second."

The doc and Andrea watched him flip through various controls before disengaging. "Easy, peasy. The only thing totally unfamiliar is the hydrogen drive, but that's basically aim-on-off, and the computer does the aiming. We're screwed if we lose that, since none of us are trained to go manual."

"I'm staying behind." Imani patted him on the shoulder and started her retreat to the door. She held her hand up when Andrea would have protested. "I'm not ditching you, I'm covering for you. This is not exactly a sanctioned use of the transpo and this is going to cost Corporate a buttload of money. If this goes wahoonie shaped, or, gods forbid, you're wrong, I'll cover your tail. I'll say you drugged me or threatened me to get my codes and you ran off station. But I'll try and delay any repo actions until we know how this is going to turn out."

"Thank you." Andrea reached out and clasped the doc's hand before she was too far away. "The rest of the chocolates and contraband in my luggage are yours. Use them wisely."

Imani snorted. "Eat them yourself when you get back." She left, closing the airlock behind her.

Brad turned to Andrea. "Are you ready?"

She settled back into her seat, trying to slow her ragged breathing. "Punch it."

They didn't find anything on the first day. Or the second. The larder was well stocked, but they kept on short rations since they didn't know how long it would take for them to find the Wave again. They spent their spare time stripping the alloy out of the trunk and applying it to the flight rig since they agreed that made more sense than diving into a chest. The autopilot was flying toward Titus and Andrea's health continued to improve from her first close encounter. Mentally, she was getting more and more frustrated. The only outside communication they had was with Serinus as they kept the doc up to date on what was happening, and Imani kept them informed on the status of the misappropriated vehicle paperwork she'd gotten wrapped up in layers of red tape.

On the third day, Andrea sighed before levering herself off the floor where she had been meditating in an effort to...she didn't really know what. Open herself? Make herself receptive? She wasn't great at explaining herself to Brad about what she was attempting. "Still nothing."

"Maybe we should turn back. I think I have enough creds built up to cover the cost of fuel and rations we've used. If we're not going to do any good out here, it just makes sense." Brad was perched on the copilot's seat, watching Andrea carefully for any sign of mental distress. He wasn't sure she wouldn't just go catatonic during another confrontation with the Wave and he wanted to be prepared.

"I know what I felt. Heard. Experienced." Andrea wrinkled her nose. "I really don't know how to describe what happened. You know."

Brad crossed his arms. "That's just it, I don't know. I'm taking it on faith, the faith of a scared little boy who wishes his mom hadn't died. And now we're chasing bogeymen across the universe."

"Hah. Cute." Andrea stretched. "But it is going to hit that station, and since it's not Corporate-owned, I doubt they have a single safe room, let alone a Canary to warn them. I won't let them be on my conscience. Not if I can help it."

"Fine, if that's the way you want it, but you can't very well go anywhere if you don't have a pilot. I should have just changed direction without even telling you. It's not like you would have noticed." Brad started to turn back to the rig, to change course regardless, and Andrea lost all semblance of calm, lunging toward him.

"Look, you—"

When she didn't continue, Brad snapped back, "You, what? Cat got your tongue?" When she didn't respond, Brad turned around to find her slack-jawed and her eyes unfocused.

"Shit." Brad wasted no time clambering into their altered rig. "Which way?"

Andrea pointed, relative up and to the right of the cabin, and Brad hurriedly translated that into actual coordinates, giving it all the hydrogen they had.

"Hello?" Andrea called, and Brad almost responded before realizing she was trying to talk to the Wave. A small bead of blood traveled down from her nose. "Can you hear me?" After a second, Andrea screamed, dropping to one knee. "Stop! STOP!"

Brad realized a few seconds late that this time she was talking to him and hit the emergency drop button on the drive, to start the process of bringing the ship to a standstill. Brad tried to disengage to go help her, but she got up, motioning him to stay put. There was no telling what would happen to him if he left the safety of the cage.

"Please, quieter, it hurts." Andrea tried to parse what she was experiencing in her own head, and failed. There was so much information, images and emotions and something almost like speech. It did, however, slow down a little bit, and it no longer felt like her brains would go shooting out of her ears.

"Do you understand me?" Andrea sat slowly and leaned back against the bulkhead, closing her eyes, as if that might help her grok the input any better.

A cascade of sensation answered her, but too fast for her to pick anything apart.

She rubbed her temples, trying to relieve some of the incoming migraine. "I'm sorry, please, can you communicate any more simply? It's just too complex." She couldn't see Brad frantically booting up every sensor array on the transpo, trying to get readings outside of the ship. They still had power, which was a first for Wavefall, so he was determined to get as many readings of their environment as he could manage.

There was a pause in the Wave's presence, and then a very slow progression of things: an image of her family's hamster, the feeling of surprise, the sound of a laboratory in full swing, and a rather dizzying impression of a fourth-dimensional cube.

"Are you drawing these out of my mind?"

A feeling of negation, disgust even.

Andrea thought for a moment, trying to figure out another way to approach the question that might get an answer. "Are the things I'm seeing and feeling my brain's way of trying to interpret what you're saying?"

Pride at the accomplishment of a child, the image of a contestant winner on an old Earth game show.

Andrea took a deep breath. She peeked out at Brad and his frantic scientific endeavor, and decided to see how much information she could get. "Okay, that's...unsettling, but better than you pawing through my memories, I guess. Why have you been attacking us?"

Confusion, a blank multiple choice test sheet, and the picture of a hamster again. There was almost a chuckle attached to the last.

"Are we the hamster in this analogy?"

A sense of indecision, a flashing sequence of hamster, mouse, beetle, ant, microbe, and a sense of continuation. "Wait, we're less than microscopic. Do you mean, you haven't even been aware of us until now?"

Again, the sense of pride, the image of the winning contestant.

"So..." Andrea started, then stopped. "Then what are you doing in our universe? If it's not an attack?"

An image of test tubes, being meticulously labeled. A sense of questioning.

"You're collecting samples. Looking for something?"

Indecision and a stuttering image of someone waving their hand back and forth.

"Just looking?"

Participation ribbons, first place trophies, an old joke about mathematicians ending in, 'Close enough for all practical purposes.'

"Well, in case you didn't know, your 'just looking' has killed or disappeared—how many now, Brad?" Andrea opened her eyes again.

Brad made a quick inquiry of the ship's computer. "2,789, make that 2,791 including the two we lost this week."

Andrea waited for the Wave's reply, but as the silence stretched on, she came to a realization. "You can't hear him, can you?"

Questioning. An image of a single person in the middle of a wasteland.

"I'm the only person you can hear in this universe. Right. Well, you've killed nearly three thousand of my people. A lot of dead Canaries in there."

Sorrow. Immense, terrible, overwhelming sorrow. And guilt. Images of wrecked cars, terrorist attacks, mass graves. Andrea couldn't stop herself from tearing up in response.

"Please, please, quieter, it hurts."

The sorrow didn't let up, but the images stopped.

Andrea sighed, and realized she was crying blood once again. "You didn't know. You didn't know we were intelligent, like you."

Violent negation. No image this time. And then it was gone.

Andrea took a few deep breaths before wiping her face on her sleeve. She grimaced at the blood streaking her shirt, but hauled herself to her feet. "It's okay, it's gone now. You can get out of the rig. Could you see anything on any of the sensors?"

Brad disengaged himself and waited a moment to make sure he wasn't going to pass out before walking over to Andrea and helping her to the copilot's chair. "Well, you were right. Let me eat that humble pie first. You can talk to it, you can sense it. And since we retained power, I got some interesting readings. There was a lot of electromagnetic activity, noise on the spectrum. I'm not sure what we'll find when we get the data back for proper analysis."

Andrea rolled her head back and forth, trying to dispel the tension in her neck muscles. "That's something more than we had before."

"Did you get a sense of where it was going?"

"I don't know, it seemed pretty upset to know that it was killing people. But I feel like to be on the safe side we should dock at Titus." She groaned and peeled herself out of the chair. "But while you get us there, I need a wash and a coffee. And lots and lots of painkillers."

══°°° °══° °══ ══°°

When they got to the station, they saw that their warning had been taken seriously and most of the docking bays were empty. It did not take long to get clearance and park the ship.

They were met by the station master and a small party of concerned citizens who wanted to know what ship was foolish enough to dock at a space station under active threat from the Wave. The fact that they weren't all cowering in the safe room was a testament to their bravery or foolishness.

The SM didn't even wait for them to step out of the airlock before pouncing. "Are you sure? How do you know?"

Andrea shrugged. "Hello to you, too. And I talked to it. Twice now."

"You've got to be kidding me. You caused a panic, young lady, emptied half the station for no good godsdamned reason—"

Brad cut him off. "Your sensors couldn't pick it up from over here, but it was just out there. I know, because it finally let our sensors stay on for once so we know what it looks like— electromagnetically, at least. We're not sure what it's going to do now that it knows it was carrying off sentient creatures, but I wouldn't bet on it staying gone for long."

The station master had just opened his mouth to retort when Andrea clapped her hands over her ears, even though Brad knew it didn't actually do anything to block out the whining hum of the approaching Wave. "Incoming, folks!"

The Canary standing just behind the station master collapsed to the floor and started convulsing, the antenna on his skin flashing red, and a moment later the ship's Wave alarm cried out, creating a pulsing throb with the hum in her own head. Brad bent down and scooped up the young Canary behind the station master and hollered, "MOVE, people. T-minus five. Git!"

They sprinted down the halls of the station, slewing around corners, and Andrea bent to help one fallen woman who spun out at a turn. The group slammed through the doors to the oxygen chamber, along with a few other groups of people from around the station. It was a tight fit, but everyone made it in. Andrea stood in the doorway, listening to the hum build until it crested into ideas and words again, just as the power in the station went down.

The people in the room behind her cried out when the lights died, and they hunkered down, prepared to lose consciousness—but this time, nobody did. The Wave was behaving itself.

"What's it saying?" Brad hissed.

"Hush, I'm...lots of apologies. Lots of apologies. Images of a board of angry people, a corporate board? No, scientific review board. Oh, I think it's in a lot of trouble for not realizing we were sentient earlier. And now it's...it's asking what we need to survive?" The images and sensations streaming through her head were urgent now and she wasn't quite sure how to respond to it. "Food, water, companionship, air..."

"Pressure, love, don't forget pressure. Tell it we need to stay inside this tin can," piped a shaky voice from the back of the room.

Andrea nodded, already feeling the chill in the air as the heaters remained without power. "Right, on a planet that we specify or within one of our ships or stations like this one."

Relief. A surge of humming...and a person was standing beside her. Naked, unresponsive, but undoubtedly alive.

"Holy fuck!" Brad jumped out into the corridor and grabbed the man and towed him into the safe room just as another two more people appeared.

"Wait, wait, wait!" Andrea hollered.

Questioning images assaulted her, did it get something wrong?

"No, you got it right, but we don't have the facilities here to handle what I think you're about to do. Um, ideas folks? I think all our missing people are coming back through."

"All of them?" That was the station master this time, faint with the thought of hundreds of people needing clothing and medical attention on his station all at once. You could hear his budget going to hell in his voice.

"Yeah, I think so." A few of the more brave station residents pulled the two new unresponsive people into the chamber and started sourcing them coats and things to keep them warm.

"Send them back to an inner system planet." The station master was firm in his decision, daring anyone to argue. "They have the best resources to handle it."

"Right. Can you carry our people back to the inner system?" She pictured a map of Corporate's reach in space, with a line from where they were to the home worlds. "Look for hospitals. Um..." She pictured large industrial buildings, sickness, health, surgery, red crosses, everything she could think of having to do with hospitals. "Did that get through?"

It seemed appalled and pushed the ideas back at her and she swore it was asking, "This is how you treat your ill?"

The people behind her in the room were following the conversation, enraptured, probably wondering what the other half was saying. "Yeah, well, we have come a long way, but we don't really have anything better at the moment."

Nobel prizes, excited scientists, "Eureka!" in scrawling Technicolor comic print.

It was promising something better, new science. And then it was gone. The lights flickered back on as the generators could fill the battery again and the radiation captures started feeding into the now empty capacitors.

It was silent for a moment or two as everyone took stock of their own limbs and functional brains, and the moment was broken as the Canary sat up and looked around himself. "Wait, I made it through? Someone brought me..." Brad gave a little wave to the kid to acknowledge him, then turned back to Andrea.

"So, you realize you just sent the Wave into the most densely populated area of the universe, right?"

"Yeah, I guess I did." Andrea slumped to the floor, sucking down deep breaths with her head between her knees. Oxygen, she just needed a little bit more oxygen is all. Good thing they were still in the oxygen room and no one showed any signs of wanting to leave just yet.

Brad crouched down beside her and whispered. "Without any warning."

"*Shit*!" She tried to jump up too quickly and Brad had to steady her. "SM! I need the high priority to Corporate. Instant facetime, now!" She bolted out of the room, sprinting down the corridors and following signs to the bridge.

The station master started jogging resolutely after her. "Do you know how much that's going to *cost*?!" Their footsteps faded down the corridor and Brad shook his head, grinning.

━ ° ° °   ° ━ °   ° ━   ━ ° °

" 's that your better half just left?" It was the same voice that had reminded Andrea to ask for a pressurized environment just a few minutes ago. Brad looked down at a wizened human being of indeterminate age and gender wearing a barkeep's apron, with a towel over their shoulder.

Brad offered the elder his arm to balance them as they stepped across the threshold of the oxygen room bulkheads. "Better? I definitely think so. Mine? You're fooling yourself if you think she could belong to anyone but herself, old timer. But maybe she'll let me tag along for a little bit longer." The old timer patted his hand and released him, leaving Brad to follow sedately down the corridor after the Canary.

This book is laid out using
**Athelas** by José Scaglione and Veronika Burian  from TypeTogether
and LIBRARY 3AM by Igor Kosinsky from Bēhance.
Cover image sourced from Shutterstock and
created by DutchScenery
Printed in the USA by KDP and Amazon.

Made in the USA
Lexington, KY
28 October 2019